ARTHUR'S PEN PAL

An I Can Read Book®

ARTHUR'S PEN PAL

Story and Pictures by
Lillian Hoban

■ HarperTrophy®
A Division of HarperCollins Publishers

HarperCollins®, ✎®, Harper Trophy®, and I Can Read Book®
are trademarks of HarperCollins Publishers Inc.

Arthur's Pen Pal
Copyright © 1976 by Lillian Hoban
All rights reserved.
Manufactured in China.
For information address HarperCollins Children's Books,
a division of HarperCollins Publishers, 10 East 53rd Street, New York, NY 10022.

Library of Congress Catalog Card Number: 75-6289
ISBN 0-06-444032-X (pbk.)

10 11 12 13 SCP 20

For Julsa

It was Sunday night.

Mother and Father

had gone out to dinner.

The baby-sitter

was watching television.

Violet was doing her homework.

She drew a picture

of a cow eating grass.

"Arthur," she said, "will you

help me with my homework?

Will you help me show

how milk is made?"

"I can't," said Arthur. "I am
writing a letter to my pen pal."
"Who is your pen pal?" asked Violet.
"His name is Sandy," said Arthur,
"and he has a big brother."

"There is a girl in my class
named Sandy," said Violet.

"My pen pal is a boy,"
said Arthur.

"He is learning karate
and he plays the drums."

"Will you help me after you write
to your pen pal?" asked Violet.
"Why do you always need help?"
asked Arthur. "Little sisters
are a pain."
"Violet!" called the baby-sitter.
"It is time to take your bath."

10

Violet finished her homework.

She put her pencils and eraser

in her pencil case.

She laid out a clean dress

and a ribbon for her hair.

Then she went to take her bath.

Arthur finished writing his letter.

He wrote,

Dear Sandy,

I am glad you are my pen pal.

I have a little sister.

I wish I had a little brother.

I wish I had drums.

Send me a picture of yourself.

Your friend,

Arthur

Arthur looked in his pocket
for Sandy's address.

He pulled out two bottle caps,

a baseball card,

and some marbles.

He pulled out some string

and some chewed chewing gum.

He pulled out a rubber snake

and half of

a melted chocolate bar.

"Arthur!" called the baby-sitter.

"Get ready for bed."

15

"I can't," said Arthur.

"I am looking for something."

Arthur picked up his notebook

and shook it.

Orange peels,

a bird's feather,

a sandwich bag,

and the letter from his pen pal

fell out.

"Arthur," said the baby-sitter,

"you clean up this mess right now!

Why can't you be neat

like your little sister?"

Arthur picked up the letter
from his pen pal.

"My pen pal doesn't have

a little sister," said Arthur.

"My pen pal has a big brother.

His big brother does karate with him

and has lots of fun."

Violet came back from her bath.

"Will you play a game with us?"

she asked the baby-sitter.

"All right," said the baby-sitter.

"But first,

Arthur has to pick up his things."

"I bet my pen pal

doesn't even need a baby-sitter,"

said Arthur. "Only little sisters

need baby-sitters."

Arthur picked up his things.

Then he went to take his bath.

He ran a lot of water

into the bathtub.

He dipped his toes in the water

and washed the middle of his face

and some of his fingers.

Then he put on his pajamas

and went into the kitchen.

Violet and the baby-sitter

were playing tiddly-winks.

"Tiddly-winks is no fun," said Arthur.

"Let's Indian wrestle."

"All right," said Violet. "If you

promise not to squeeze too hard."

"Arthur," said the baby-sitter,

"let me see your hands."

"What for?" asked Arthur.

"If I see your palms,

I can tell your fortune."

23

"Hmm," said the baby-sitter.

"I see that you will get a letter
from a short, dark woman. I also see
that your hands are very dirty.

Now, go get washed."

"I bet if my pen pal
needs a baby-sitter,

he gets a *nice* one," said Arthur.

"I think she is a very nice
baby-sitter," said Violet.

"Little sisters always like
their baby-sitters," said Arthur,
and he went to get washed.

When Arthur got back,

Violet was standing on her hands.

"Why are you doing that?"

asked Arthur. "I thought

we were going to Indian wrestle."

"We will," said Violet. "But first
I have to make my arms stronger."
"What for?" asked Arthur.
"So I can beat you," said Violet.

Then Violet rolled up a newspaper.

"Now what are you doing?"

asked Arthur.

"I have to make my hands stronger,"

said Violet, "so I can squeeze you

harder than you squeeze me."

"Squeezing is no fair," said Arthur.

"I know," said Violet. "But you
always do it."

She squeezed the newspaper
as hard as she could.

"O.K.," said Violet. "Now I am ready."

29

Arthur and Violet

began to Indian wrestle.

Violet pushed Arthur's arm

as hard as she could,

but Arthur pushed harder.

Violet squeezed Arthur's hand

as hard as she could,

but Arthur squeezed harder.

"Ouch!" cried Violet.

"Arthur!" called the baby-sitter.

"Stop that right now!"

"My thumb hurts," said Violet.

"Arthur twisted it."

"Why can't you be a nice
big brother?" said the baby-sitter.
"Why do you have to hurt
your little sister?"

"Little sisters are no fun,"
said Arthur.

"They are always getting hurt.
It must be nice to have
a little brother like Sandy."

"It's not fair," said Violet.

"We always play games

where I have to be strong.

Why can't we play something

I am good at?

Why don't we skip rope?

I could beat you at

Sweet Milk, Sour Milk

or Red Hot Pepper any day."

"That is a very good idea,"
said the baby-sitter. "But now
it is time for bed."
"O.K.," said Arthur,
"but I bet I can beat Violet
at rope skipping.

And I bet my pen pal
and his big brother
could beat Violet too."
"We'll see," said Violet,
and they both went to bed.

The next day,

Arthur mailed the letter

to his pen pal.

When Arthur got home,

Violet had the skipping rope ready.

"Shall we start on the easy skipping,

like Sweet Milk, Sour Milk?

Or do you want to go right for

Red Hot Pepper?"

"Let me practice first," said Arthur.

He skipped slow and he skipped fast.

He skipped Sweet Milk, Sour Milk

and he skipped Red Hot Pepper.

"That's not bad," said Violet.

"Now, let's see you do this."

She skipped Sweet Milk, Sour Milk.

When she came to Buttermilk, Skim,

she skipped the rope so high

that Arthur couldn't believe it!

Then Violet skipped Red Hot Pepper.

She skipped,

> Vinegar, mustard,
>
> pepper, salt.
>
> Chili sauce and pickles,
>
> onions mixed with malt.
>
> Catsup, ketchup,
>
> Red Hot Pepper!

When she came to Catsup, ketchup,

she skipped very fast.

When she came to Red Hot Pepper,

she skipped very *very* fast. And she

looped-the-loop at the same time!

"O.K.," said Violet. "Now *you* do it."

Arthur took a deep breath.

He held the rope tight.

First he skipped slowly.

When he came to Catsup, ketchup,

he skipped faster.

Then he came to Red Hot Pepper.

He skipped very very fast.

But when he tried to loop-the-loop,

his foot got caught and he fell down.

"Well, Mister Smarty-pants,"
said Violet. "Maybe I can't beat you
at Indian wrestling,
but I can beat you
at rope skipping.
And I bet I could beat your pen pal
and his big brother too!"
"My pen pal doesn't skip rope,"
said Arthur.
"My pen pal is strong
and so is his brother.
They Indian wrestle
and do karate.

I wish I were my pen pal's
big brother," said Arthur.
"And I am going to write a letter
to my pen pal
and tell him so!"

Arthur wrote another letter

to his pen pal.

He wrote,

Dear Sandy,

I wish I were your big brother.

Then we could Indian wrestle.

Or maybe do karate.

All my little sister can do

is skip rope.

She thinks she is great

because she can loop-the-loop

and do Red Hot Pepper

at the same time.

Don't forget to send me your picture.

                    Your friend,

                    Arthur

At the end of the week,

Arthur got a letter from his pen pal.

It said,

Dear Arthur,

I love to Indian wrestle.

I always win because

I am the All-Girls' Champ.

Tell me more about

your little sister.

I can double loop-the-loop

while I do Red Hot Pepper.

Can she?

Here is the picture you asked for.

The one on the floor

is my big brother.

Your friend,

Sandy

P.S. My big brother says

he will trade places with you any day.

Arthur looked at the picture
for a long time.

He read the letter again.

He looked at the picture some more.

Arthur thought about little sisters

and big brothers for a long time.

He thought about

his little sister, Violet.

53

She did not cry too much

when he beat her

at Indian wrestling.

She did not brag too much

when she beat him at rope skipping.

And she *never* knocked him down,
because she couldn't *do* karate!

Then Arthur wrote
another letter to Sandy.
He wrote,

Dear Sandy,

I like the way you look

in your karate outfit.

Does your brother like having

a little sister who does karate?

My little sister is pretty neat.

She *can* double loop-the-loop

while she does Red Hot Pepper.

And she can even do it BACKWARDS!

Your friend,

Arthur

P.S. Tell your brother

I don't want to trade places.

When the baby-sitter came again,

Violet said, "We had

a rope-skipping contest,

and I won."

"Well," said the baby-sitter,

"I guess Arthur is better

at Indian wrestling,

and you are better at rope skipping."

"Yes," said Arthur.

"Violet can skip Red Hot Pepper
and loop-the-loop at the same time.
And I bet she can even
double loop-the-loop
and skip Red Hot Pepper."

"I CAN!" said Violet.

"How did you know?"

"I got a letter
from a short, dark woman,"
said Arthur.

"Sandy?" asked Violet.

"Yes," said Arthur.

"Well," said the baby-sitter,
"maybe I should tell fortunes
instead of baby-sitting."

"Oh no," said Violet. "I like having you for a baby-sitter."

"So do I," said Arthur.

"I always knew you did,"
said the baby-sitter.
And she gave them both
a big hug.